Lauren and Val
Take a Walk

Lauren and Val Take a Walk

A BEST FRIENDS BOOK

Written by
Lauren Eileen

Illustrated by
Hanne Brøter

HIGHLANDER
PRESS

Hardback ISBN: 978-1-7372638-6-9
Paperback ISBN: 978-1-7372638-5-2
Library of Congress Control Number: 2021947865

Published by Highlander Press
501 W. University Pkwy, Ste. B2
Baltimore, MD 21210
www.highlanderpressbooks.com

Author's photo credit: Shawna Shenette Photography
Illustrator's photo credit: B.T. Stokke

The illustrations in this book were created digitally using Adobe Photoshop and Wacom Cintiq 16.
Text and title font: Andika New Basic.

A portion of the sales from this book will benefit the
North Shore Alliance for GLBTQ+ Youth (NAGLY), located in Salem Massachusetts.

For Val,
my best friend

Lauren and Val
are best friends.

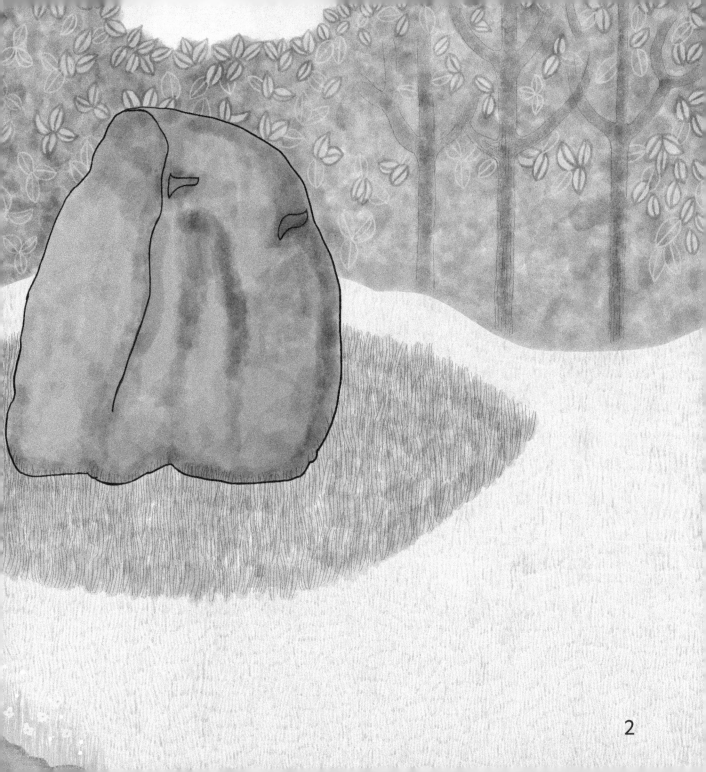

"My tummy is rumbling," says Val.

"Mine too," says Lauren. "Let's get lunch!"

3

"Goodbye balloon!" yells Lauren.

"Ooooooohhhhhh," Val gasps.

4

"Look!"
exclaims Lauren.

"There's so much to see,"
says Val.

5

"WOOF!" barks the golden pooch.

"Have fun girls," says the jogger.

6

Down the road a bit, Lauren whispers,
"Wow, butterflies."

"These flowers smell so good," Val says.

"I can tell!"
giggles Lauren

Rounding a corner, the girls
meet two mothers out for
a walk with their baby.

"Hi, baby.
I like your
red stroller,"
says Val.

"Have a great
day, girls," says
one of the moms.

"What's that sound?"
Lauren asks.

11

"Good luck—be safe,"
Val yells over the siren.

12

At the bottom of a hill, Lauren and Val come to the Post Office.

13

"It's a nice day for a walk!"
 says the letter carrier.

"It sure is," says Val.

14

"Close your eyes and smell that freshly baked bread," says Val.

15

"Welcome, girls.
I hope you're hungry!"
says the cook.

"We sure are!"
calls Lauren

16

Just as the girls are about to bite into
their toasted BLT sandwiches, they hear a loud,
"MEOOOOWWWWW."

"Say hello to Murray!"
calls the cook.
"He's the real boss of this place."

Val giggles and says, "Hello, kitty."

Walking slowly, the girls
make their way back
to the big rock where
they started their afternoon.

19

"We've seen so many interesting things on our walk,"
Val says to Lauren. "What has been your favorite part of the day?"

Lauren thinks for a few seconds
before replying,
"Spending it with you."

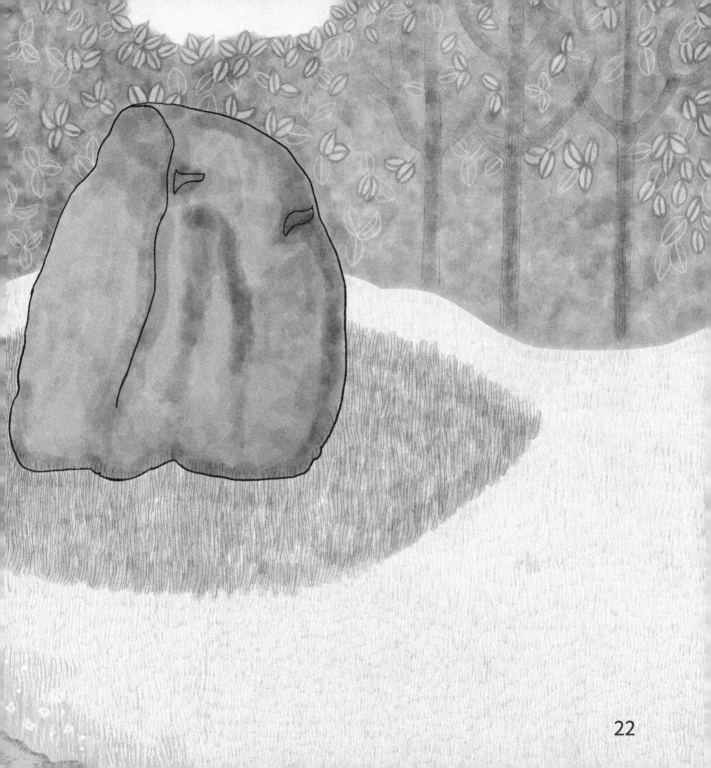

About the Author

Lauren Eileen searched in vain in children's literature trying to find herself, and her LGBTQ+ community, represented on the page. So, she wrote the kind of inclusive and loving stories she sought, using her more than forty-year real-life friendship with Valerie as a foundation.

She lives with her teenaged son, Anthony, and her partner, Maze, in Massachusetts, where they enjoy staying active. Her favorite thing to do is laugh. *Lauren and Val Take a Walk* is her first book.

www.laureneileenauthor.com

About the Illustrator

Hanne Brøter is a Norwegian illustrator and graphic designer.
She wrote and illustrated her own children's book
Senza Ratio & Madame Bonsens Travel Into Space in 2016, and has illustrated the book *Good Night Farm* (2019) by Kathleen Vallejos.

www.yourbrandvision.com

ABOUT THE PUBLISHER

Highlander Press, founded in 2019, is a mid-sized publishing company committed to diversity and sharing big ideas thereby changing the world through words.

Highlander Press guides authors from where they are in the writing-editing-publishing process to where they have an impactful book of which they are proud, making a long-time dream come true. Having authored a book improves your confidence, helps create clarity, and ensures that you claim your expertise.

What makes Highlander Press unique is that their business model focuses on building strong collaborative relationships with other women-owned businesses, which specialize in some aspect of the publishing industry, such as graphic design, book marketing, book launching, copyrights, and publicity. The mantra "a rising tide lifts all boats" is one they embrace. https://highlanderpressbooks.com

f facebook.com/highlanderpress

instagram.com/highlanderpress

in linkedin.com/in/highlanderpress

Helplines/Websites:

- **Trevor Lifeline** is a crisis intervention and suicide prevention phone service **available 24/7 for LGBTQ+ youth at 1-866-488-7386.**

- **Q Chat Space** is a bully-free online community of LGBTQ teens that can chat with other LGBTQ teens and trained staff from LGBTQ centers around the country. You can access Q Chat Space at www.qchatspace.org.

- **The LGBT National Help Center** offers a talk-line and weekly chatrooms for youth, providing confidential peer-support, information, local resources and community. You can call the LGBT National Youth Talk-line at 800-246-7743.

- You can access the **Weekly Youth Chatrooms** at glbthotline.org/youthchatrooms.

About NAGLY

The North Shore Alliance of GLBTQ+ Youth, located in Salem, Massachusetts, is dedicated to honoring, respecting, educating, and empowering GLBTQ youth by providing a safe place to gather, learn, heal, and grow. Learn more at https://www.nagly.org/.

9 781737 263869